AF526350

My
Little Christmas
Treasury

My Little Christmas Treasury

Little Christmas Animals
One Tiny Baby
The Best Thing About Christmas

A Happy Day® Books Gift Collection

An Inspirational Press Book for Children

Previously published in three separate volumes:

LITTLE CHRISTMAS ANIMALS
Copyright © 1994 by The Standard Publishing Company

ONE TINY BABY
Copyright © 1989 by The Standard Publishing Company

THE BEST THING ABOUT CHRISTMAS
Text Copyright © 1990 by Christine Harder Tangvald
Illustrations Copyright © 1990 by The Standard Publishing Company

All rights reserved. No part of this work may be reproduced or transmitted in any form or by any means, electronic or mechanical, including photocopying, recording, or any information storage and retrieval system, without permission in writing from The Standard Publishing Company, 8121 Hamilton Avenue, Cincinnati, Ohio 45231.

First Inspirational Press edition published in 2000.

Inspirational Press
A division of BBS Publishing Corporation
386 Park Avenue South
New York, NY 10016

Inspirational Press is a registered trademark of BBS Publishing Corporation.

This edition published by arrangement with Standard Publishing of 8121 Hamilton Avenue, Cincinnati, Ohio 45231.

Library of Congress Control Number: 99-71874

ISBN: 0-88486-261-5

Printed in China.

Little Christmas Animals

Henrietta D. Gambill
illustrated by Kathy Parks

To John, Matthew, Kelsey, and Griffin
with love

Little Goat lived in Nazareth, at Mary’s house.
One day he heard a strange sound . . .

Swoosh! A shiny angel had appeared.
Mary was surprised!

Little Goat watched as the angel talked to Mary. *What's he telling her?* wondered Little Goat.

Little Donkey lived in a barn near Mary's house.
His mother lived there too.

One day Little Donkey saw Mary climb upon his mother's back. Joseph helped her. "Now we are ready to go to Bethlehem," said Joseph. *Why are they going to Bethlehem?* wondered Little Donkey.

Little Camel rested beside the dusty road. She was traveling to Bethlehem in a caravan of travelers and merchants.

Little Camel saw Mary
and Joseph coming
toward the caravan.

Are they going to Bethlehem with us?
wondered Little Camel.

Little Parrot sat on her perch at the Bethlehem inn, watching the travelers.

One day Little Parrot saw Mary and Joseph come to the inn. *That lady looks like she is going to have a baby* ***soon,*** thought Little Parrot.

Little Ox lived in the stable near the inn. He stopped munching hay when Mary and Joseph came into the stable.

Joseph began to fill a manger with clean hay. He was in a hurry. He talked softly to Mary. *She's having a baby!* Little Ox said to himself. *Will the baby be born in **my** stable?*

Little Calf stood near Little Ox. They were friends. Little Calf and Little Ox watched as Mary put her newborn baby in the manger filled with hay. Joseph helped her. They looked happy!

Little Calf moved closer to the manger.
What's the baby's name? he wondered.

Little Lamb snuggled close to her mother on the hillside. She was *so* sleepy. She listened to the shepherds talking softly.

Suddenly a bright, shiny angel appeared! “Go to Bethlehem,” the angel said. “A special baby has been born. You will find him in a manger.” *What does the baby look like?* wondered Little Lamb.

Little Sheep Dog saw the angel too. Then more angels from heaven appeared in the sky. . .

. . . lots and lots of angels!
They began to praise God.
The shepherds were not afraid anymore.
“Let’s go to Bethlehem,” they said.
Are we going to see the baby?
wondered Little Sheep Dog.

Little Dove saw the shepherds hurrying to Bethlehem. She flew quickly to catch up with them. They were talking about finding a baby in a manger.

I saw a baby in a stable in Bethlehem, thought Little Dove. *Is that the baby they are going to see?*

Little Pony stood near the manger. He saw the shepherds come into the stable.

They were happy to find the baby. “An angel told us we would find baby Jesus here,” they said.

Will the shepherds tell everyone that Jesus has been born? wondered Little Pony.

When the shepherds left the stable, they did tell everyone about the baby in the manger.

But all the animals wondered. Do we have to wonder too? No. Just like the shepherds, we know who he was — little baby Jesus, God's own Son.

One Tiny Baby

written by Mark A. Taylor

illustrated by Kathryn Hutton

One tiny baby—
See Him on the hay?

Two smiling people—
Hear Mary say,

“We are very happy
with this little one.
His name is Jesus,
God’s only Son.”

Three fuzzy donkeys
may have rested there.

Or four nosy puppies
may have sniffed the air.

Five sleepy cows
may have wondered why

Their quiet stable
heard a baby's cry.

Six woolly lambs
may have watched to see

Seven strong men
falling on their knees.

"This must be Jesus,"
the happy shepherds say.

"Many angels told us
He was born today."

Eight cooing doves,
perched overhead,

Also see the baby
in His manger bed.

Nine busy spiders,
  spinning webs with care,

Pay no attention
to Jesus sleeping there.

But ten noisy roosters,
when the night is done,
Seem to crow together,
"God has sent His Son!"

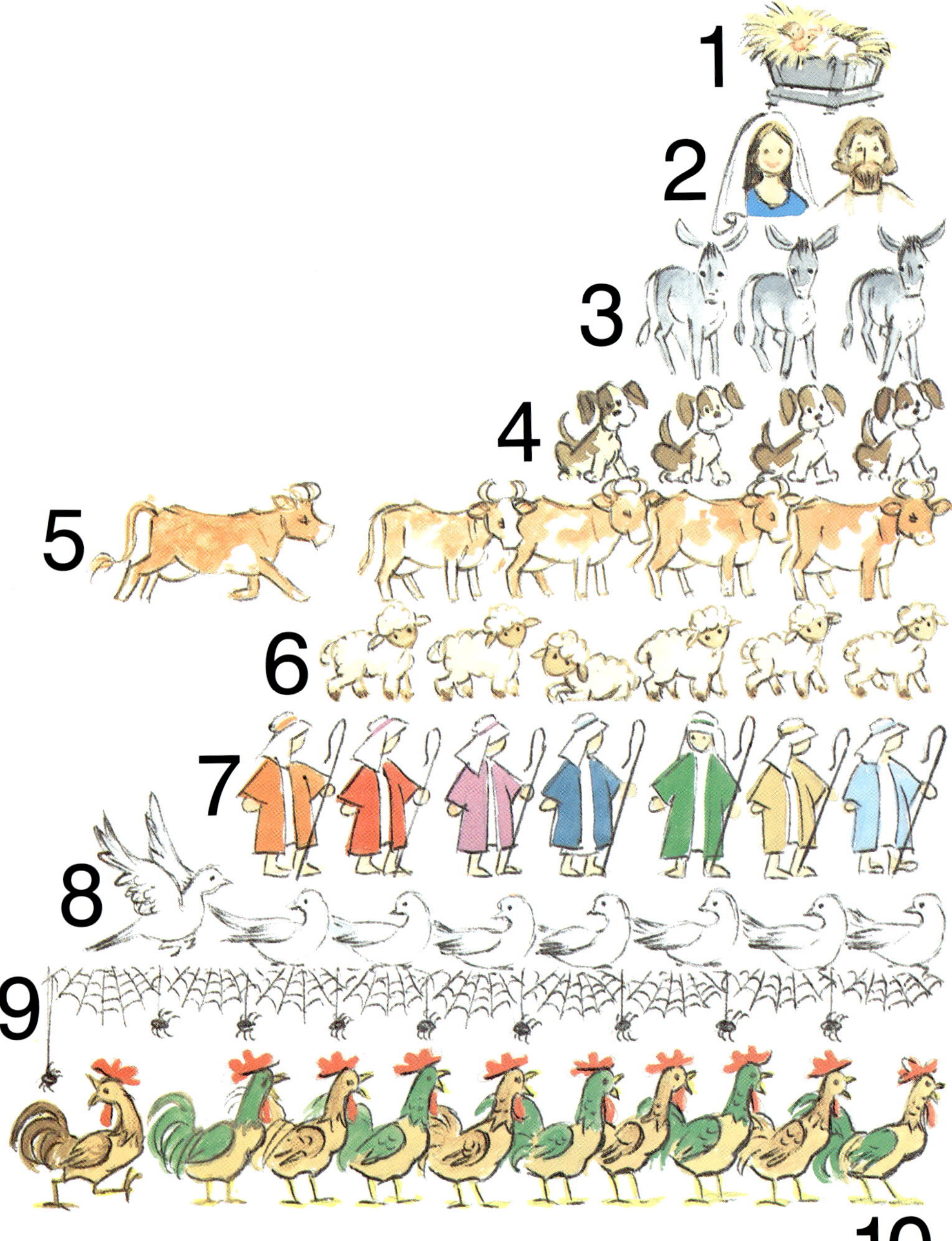

10

The BEST Thing About Christmas

written by Christine Harder Tangvald

illustrated by Judy Hand

I like everything about Christmas, don't you?

I like to decorate our Christmas tree with silver tinsel, and pretty ornaments, and tiny lights that wink and blink, blink and wink.

And I like to put shiny round balls on our Christmas tree — red ones, and blue ones, and green ones, and yellow ones.

Decorating our Christmas tree is fun.

But that's not the BEST thing about Christmas.

I like all the colors
of Christmas.

Blue and green packages
tied with bows made
of satin ribbon,

and snowy
white candles
to light with
a match,

and bright yellow stars that twinkle
and shine through the night,

and striped red candy canes stuffed
in our Christmas stockings. Oh, yes.
I like the colors of Christmas.

But that's not the BEST thing about Christmas.

I like all the special words we use at Christmas.

"Ho, Ho, HO!"

and

"JOY to the world!"

and

"MERRY CHRISTMAS, everyone!"

And I like all the things people do at Christmas to help other people.

We care and share. We shake hands and smile and say, “Hello! How ARE you? It’s so good to see you.”

It makes me feel good when I care and share with other people.

But that’s not the BEST thing about Christmas.

I like all the good foods to eat at Christmas.

Pretty sugar cookies with red and green frosting and sprinkles on the top. Yum, yum, YUM!

And turkey with dressing and cranberry sauce and pumpkin pie with lots of whipped cream for dessert. Yum, yum, YUM!

And big round oranges,

and chocolate fudge,

and gooey, chewy gumdrops! YUM, YUM, YUM!
I love gooey, chewy gumdrops!

But that's not the BEST thing about Christmas.

I like the sounds of Christmas.
Christmas bells ringing DING, DONG, DING!
People singing—
FA, la la la LA, la LA, LA, LA!

And I like the smells of Christmas.

The fresh smell of our pine wreath hanging on the front door, and the smell of Mom's apple pie baking in the oven.
Mmmmmmm. Mmmmmmm. Good.

But that's still not the BEST thing about Christmas.

And I like the time we spend together at Christmas.

Eating together,

shopping together,

reading together,

praying together,

and just talking together.

Being together at Christmas is nice.
But that's not the BEST thing about Christmas, either!
Then what IS the best thing about Christmas?

I think the BEST thing about Christmas is . . .

JESUS!
BABY JESUS!

Yes, Jesus is the best thing about Christmas. You see, Christmas is Jesus' birthday. And did you know that Jesus is God's own Son? He is. He is God's very own Son.

Long ago, baby Jesus was born in a stable in a little town called Bethlehem. Mary was Jesus' mother. Joseph was there, too. He took good care of Mary and baby Jesus. It was God's plan.

That first Christmas night, God sent beautiful angels to tell the shepherds about his Son, Jesus. "Glory to God in the highest!" sang the angels.

The shepherds were surprised, and . . .

. . . they left their flocks of sheep out in the fields and came to Bethlehem to worship Jesus.

The shepherds loved baby Jesus.

And did you know that Jesus came into this world for me, too? He did. He really, really did. Isn't that wonderful? Jesus came for me.

Thank you, God, for Christmas.
Happy birthday, Jesus.

Yes, I like everything about Christmas.
But I think the BEST thing is . . .

. . . Jesus came for ME!